Meet
Angelina Ballerina™

Based on the stories by Katharine Holabird
Based on the illustrations by Helen Craig

SIMON SPOTLIGHT
New York London Toronto Sydney New Delhi

SIMON SPOTLIGHT

An imprint of Simon & Schuster Children's Publishing Division
1230 Avenue of the Americas, New York, New York 10020 • This Simon Spotlight edition May 2020 • Illustrated by Robert McPhillips
© 2020 Helen Craig Ltd and Katharine Holabird. The Angelina Ballerina name and character and the dancing Angelina logo
are trademarks of HIT Entertainment Limited, Katharine Holabird, and Helen Craig. All rights reserved, including the right of
reproduction in whole or in part in any form. SIMON SPOTLIGHT and colophon are registered trademarks of Simon & Schuster,
Inc. For information about special discounts for bulk purchases, please contact
Simon & Schuster Special Sales at 1-866-506-1949 or business@simonandschuster.com.
Manufactured in the United States of America 0320 LAK • 10 9 8 7 6 5 4 3 2 1
ISBN 978-1-5344-4250-4 • ISBN 978-1-5344-4251-1 (eBook)

Angelina Ballerina lives in the charming Mouseland village of Chipping Cheddar.

Angelina starts each day the same way—dancing! She practices pliés in her bedroom.

She practices leaps
in the living room.

She practices twirls in the kitchen.

"Angelina, please be careful!" says her mother. Angelina and her little sister Polly are helping their parents make cheddar pies for a picnic. Today, Angelina and her family are going to the summer festival in Chipping Cheddar!

"Don't forget your dance class," Angelina's father reminds her.

Later, Angelina picks up her
bag and twirls out the door.
"We'll meet you at the
festival!" her mom says.

Angelina is *very* excited for the festival. The Royal Ballet is performing. Angelina can't wait to see all the ballerinas dance onstage!

Angelina dances down the street so fast that she bumps into her neighbor, Mrs. Hodgepodge.

"Watch out, Angelina!" scolds Mrs. Hodgepodge.

"Oops! Sorry, Mrs. Hodgepodge!" says Angelina, then she leaps and spins all the way to Miss Lilly's Ballet School.

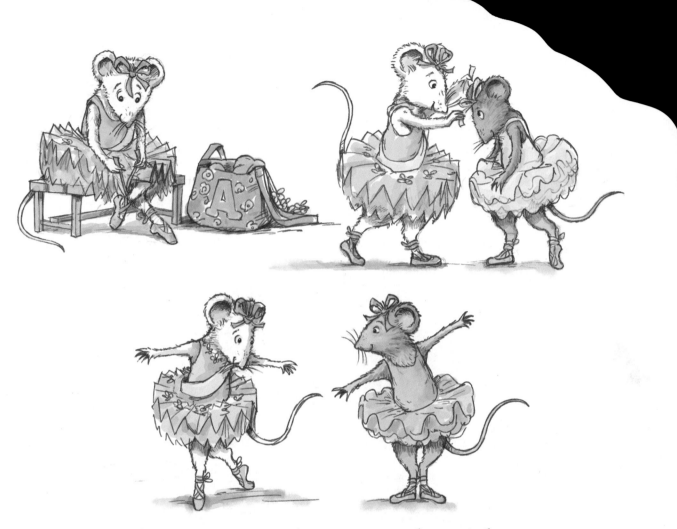

As soon as she arrives, Angelina puts on her pink tutu
and ballet slippers. Then she helps Flora tie her bow and
she does warm-up stretches with her best friend, Alice.

Miss Quaver gets ready to play the piano in the studio. Miss Lilly smiles and says, "Take your places at the barre, little dancers."

Miss Quaver begins to play, and the ballet lesson starts. Angelina loves dancing to the music as she follows Miss Lilly's directions.

"Let's begin in first position," Miss Lilly tells the class.

Angelina and her friends have lots of fun practicing ballet steps together.

Flora leaps in the air and does a grand jeté.
Felicity practices her pliés.
Angelina and Alice do lovely arabesques.
"Splendid!" Miss Lilly cheers.

Angelina's little cousin Henry tries to do an arabesque too, but he falls over and stubs his toe.

"Ouch!" cries Henry.

"Oh no!" says Angelina, and she takes Henry to see kind Dr. Tuttle.

"Your toe will be fine," says Dr. Tuttle with a smile. "But don't do any dancing at the summer festival!"

"I know what will make you feel better, Henry," says Angelina. "Let's visit Mrs. Thimble's shop."

Mrs. Thimble's shop is one of Angelina's favorite places in all of Chipping Cheddar!

"Everything looks so delicious!" says Angelina, looking through the shop window.

"I'm hungry!" says Henry.

Angelina and Henry join all their school friends inside the shop. Everyone is buying Mrs. Thimble's tasty cakes.

Angelina chooses a strawberry cupcake, and Henry chooses a chocolate one. They are scrumptious!

"Come on, Henry," says Angelina. "Let's go to the festival!"

Angelina and Henry meet Mr. and Mrs. Mouseling and Polly at the festival. Then they all play games and take a ride on the giant Ferris wheel!

At last it is time for the Royal Ballet performance!
Angelina loves watching the ballerinas dance gracefully
around the maypole. When the performance is over,
Angelina and Henry clap and cheer, "Hooray!"

At the end of the festival, Angelina, Henry, and her family watch dazzling fireworks light up the sky, and then they walk home together.

"What a wonderful day!" says Angelina.